The Amazing Christmas Extravaganza

DAVID SHANNON

THE BLUE SKY PRESS
An Imprint of Scholastic Inc. · New York

MERRY CHRISTMAS, HEIDI

THE BLUE SKY PRESS

Copyright © 1995 by David Shannon

Library of Congress Cataloging-in-Publication Data
Shannon, David, 1959–
The amazing Christmas extravaganza / David Shannon.
p.   cm.
Summary: Much to the dismay of his neighbors and family,
Mr. Merriweather's Christmas display grows from a simple string
of white lights into an outrageous spectacle.
ISBN 0-590-48090-1
[1. Christmas decorations — Fiction.   2. Christmas — Fiction.]
I. Title. PZ7.S52865Am 1995 [E] — dc20 94-31980 CIP AC

12 11 10 9 8 7 6 5 4 3   5 6 7 8 9/9 0/0
Printed in Singapore
First printing, October 1995

The paintings in this book were executed in acrylic.
The text type was set in Meridien Medium by WLCR New York, Inc.
Color separations were made by Bright Arts, Ltd., Singapore.
Printed and bound by Tien Wah Press, Singapore
Production supervision by Angela Biola
Designed by Kathleen Westray and David Shannon

IT ALL STARTED with one little string of tiny white
Christmas lights.

In the past, Mr. Merriweather had been happy celebrating
Christmas with his wife and their children, Matthew and Sarah.
Each year he made a big show of getting the box of ornaments
down from the attic. Then the Merriweather family decorated
the tree together and hung a wreath on the front door.

But this Christmas was different.

"This year we're really going to celebrate Christmas," he announced. "This year we're going to put lights on the house!"

They were all very excited. Mrs. Merriweather clapped her hands, and Sarah hopped on one foot.

Then Mr. Merriweather hauled his ladder outside and tacked up a small string of white lights around the front window.

"That's fine," he said, admiring his handiwork. He left the lights on all night so he could see the glow from his bedroom, and he went to sleep a happy man.

"Kind of a shrimpy little string of lights ya got there, pal."

Mr. Merriweather stopped shoveling and turned to see
Mr. Clack, his neighbor from across the street. "Wait till you
see *my* house," Mr. Clack bragged. "I got seventeen strings
of lights, and they blink on and off!"

Mr. Merriweather was suddenly embarrassed. "Well . . .
I'm not done yet. You wait till I'm finished, and then I guess
you'll see something!" He pulled his hat down over his ears
and went back to his shoveling.

That afternoon, Mr. Merriweather gathered up his kids and drove the station wagon to five big department stores. He bought so many Christmas decorations that he couldn't close the tailgate.

He could hardly wait to get home and put them all up.

"Can we really afford all that?" Mrs. Merriweather asked when she saw the decorations.

"Of course we can, honey," Mr. Merriweather said. "It's Christmas!"

That night he peeked out his bedroom window and saw Mr. Clack staring up at the new display. He chuckled to himself when Mr. Clack kicked some snow and stomped home.

The next day, all of Mr. Merriweather's neighbors stopped by to tell him how wonderful his house looked. He had never gotten so many compliments. They made him feel giddy and full inside, like he'd just eaten a big dinner. But still, he thought, there was room for improvement.

Every morning, for the next week, Mr. Merriweather fired up the old station wagon and went in search of more decorations, which he carefully added onto his house with the seriousness of a true artist. And every evening, the neighbors and their kids came out to see the new wonders sprouting from the house of lights.

"Magnificent!" the neighbors exclaimed. "Awesome!"

Matthew's and Sarah's friends told them they were lucky to have such a great dad.

"Yeah," Matthew said, a little puzzled. "He's really something."

Mrs. Merriweather tried to be understanding, but she was worried. Christmas Day would be here soon, and it seemed that her husband could only think of colored lights and plastic candles. She was relieved when Mr. Merriweather told her he had been to every store he could find, and there was nothing left to buy.

Then she heard the hammer banging and the saw buzzing in the garage. . . .

Several days later, Mr. Merriweather unveiled what he had made.
"It's truly an extravaganza!" the neighbors gasped. Mr. Merriweather
flipped a switch, and a recording of "The Twelve Days of Christmas"
blared out of loudspeakers. Life-sized wooden cutouts filled the yard,
representing each of the twelve days. There were maids-a-milking,
geese-a-laying, lords-a-leaping, and even a partridge in a pear tree.

"And this is nothing!" shouted Mr. Merriweather. "You should see what I'm building next!"

"Terrific," muttered Mr. Clack. "I like celebrating Christmas as much as the next guy, but this is ridiculous!"

Mr. Merriweather was no longer thinking about Christmas, however. He was thinking about bigger, brighter, and more.

The next night, Mr. Merriweather was back at work on his extravaganza.

"You'd better come down now, dear!" Mrs. Merriweather called up to him. "The children are in the Christmas program tonight."

"Sorry, no time!" Mr. Merriweather mumbled through a mouth full of nails. "I've got too much to do. You go on without me."

It was hopeless. Mrs. Merriweather tried to explain to Matthew and Sarah that their father was a very busy man.

"I think he's gone a little wacko," Matthew said.

"Hush!" his mother scolded. "Don't talk about your father that way."

Mr. Merriweather's display continued to grow. One day he put up Santa's workshop, complete with elves. The next day he added giant snowmen made of Styrofoam. And finally, he built a fifty-foot Santa with a mechanical arm that waved.

People from three counties away brought their children to see the now-famous Merriweather front yard. But it wasn't so much fun anymore for the people who lived nearby.

The extravaganza used so much electricity that there was hardly any left for the neighbors. Their Christmas trees were dim and dull, and their Christmas cookies came out doughy from ovens that wouldn't heat. The noise from the sightseers' honking and yelling was so loud that the annual Christmas caroling had to be canceled — no one could hear the singers. People visiting their families got stranded for hours in the tangle of traffic. Sometimes they just gave up and went home.

Mr. Merriweather didn't even notice. He sat snugly in his brightly lit home, humming along with "The Twelve Days of Christmas."

Finally, the neighbors decided something had to be done. On Christmas Eve, they held a meeting at Mr. Clack's house.

"Let's call the cops!" someone shouted.

"Let's take him to court!" screamed another.

"Now, wait a minute," said Mr. Clack. "We don't want to look like a bunch of Scrooges."

Just then, all the lights in the neighborhood went out. Up and down the street, everything was black. Everything, that is, except the Christmas Extravaganza, which glowed brighter than ever.

"That's the last straw!" roared Mr. Clack. "I don't care what people think. I say we tear it down ourselves — tonight!"

Everyone yelled in agreement. Then they armed themselves with tools of destruction and swarmed over Mr. Merriweather's front yard — slashing, bashing, and trashing everything in sight.

Mr. Merriweather and his wife woke up in midair. "Oh my, oh no!" he wailed.

"What is it?" cried the children, running into the room.

"I think it's an earthquake!" Mr. Merriweather exclaimed.

They all dove under the bed and huddled there together, listening to the terrible screeching, cracking, and thumping. It lasted all night long.

Finally, the noises stopped. Mr. Merriweather poked his head out from under the bed. It was morning — Christmas morning. He ran downstairs, opened the front door, and couldn't believe what he saw.

The Christmas Extravaganza was gone! Yesterday, giant snowflakes, Santa Clauses, reindeer, and lights had decorated his house and yard. Now, there was only a huge pile of sputtering rubble.

Mr. Clack and the rest of the mob were still standing around. Their heavy breath steamed in the cold morning air.

"I guess that'll teach you to muck up *our* neighborhood," Mr. Clack sneered.

Mr. Merriweather felt as if he'd been hit by a log. He could barely talk. "B-but I was just celebrating Christmas," he said. "I didn't know it bothered you. I thought you liked it."

The neighbors were silent. No longer caught up in their attack, they looked at each other and began to think about what they had done. And they were ashamed.

"I'm sorry," Mr. Clack said sheepishly. He picked up a pair of broken reindeer antlers. "Here," he said. "We'll help you put it all back together again. We'll make it even better!"

Mr. Merriweather shook his head. "No," he said. "I think some nice little white lights will do just fine." He pulled the tiny string out of the smoking heap, and Mr. Clack and all the neighbors helped him tack it up around the front window.

Mrs. Merriweather brought out cups of hot cider, and the whole neighborhood admired Mr. Merriweather's little string of white lights, his fine tree, and his beautiful wreath.

"You know, Mr. Merriweather," Mr. Clack said, "that really was an amazing Christmas Extravaganza."

"Thank you," replied Mr. Merriweather, "but these are my *real* masterpieces." He hugged Matthew and then swung Sarah high up into the air.

Mrs. Merriweather took her husband by the arm. "Don't feel bad, dear," she said. "Everybody should be able to celebrate Christmas in his own way, whether it's with lots of lights or none at all. Yours just got so big there wasn't room for anyone else."

"Well, I've learned my lesson," Mr. Merriweather said with a sigh. "I guess I got carried away."

"I think everyone did," Mrs. Merriweather said. "But I'm proud of you. I didn't know you were so artistic!"

Mr. Merriweather smiled. He gazed at his children, his friends, and his big mound of junk. He noticed that several large pieces of wood were still in good condition. "Hmmm," he wondered out loud. "How many days till Easter?"